Jodie

HILARY McKAY

Illustrated by
Keith Robinson

Barrington Stoke

To the Wildlife Trusts and their volunteers.

Thank you for fifty years of friendship and weather and wonderful days.

First published in 2023 in Great Britain by
Barrington Stoke Ltd
18 Walker Street, Edinburgh, EH3 7LP

www.barringtonstoke.co.uk

Text © 2023 Hilary McKay
Illustrations © 2023 Keith Robinson

A CIP catalogue record for this book is available
from the British Library upon request

ISBN: 978-1-80090-220-6

Printed by Hussar Books, Poland

CONTENTS

Chapter 1

Where I Am Now

My name is Jodie.

I'm on a school trip. We're at a field centre. That's a place where people study nature and geography and other outdoor things. Part of it is like a hostel and part is for science. Students from university come, and birdwatchers, as well as schools like ours. We are here for two nights. It's October, end of season, so it's cheap.

The staff said, "Anything you're unsure about, tell someone, don't keep quiet – any problems, any worries."

Some people are talkers, but I'm a listener. I never tell anyone anything.

They also said, "Nobody is to go anywhere alone."

But right from the start, I went out alone.

And now I'm trapped. I'm trapped in this haunted place.

Don't think I haven't tried screaming. Because I have.

This is our second day, and I heard the little dog again, barking, barking, frightened, frantic. On and on went the long bursts of barking and then single exhausted yaps: yap – pause – yap.

A longer pause each time.

Nobody did anything to help the dog. No one even seemed to hear.

But I couldn't bear it.

This is a salt marsh. Imagine mud – cold sea mud. Watery mud, reflecting the sky. Ancient mud. Mud split into jigsaw-puzzle pieces by creeks filled with water.

In places, patches of small plants grow in the mud. They have stiff grey-green leaves, and stems like wire. These plants are drowned twice every day because the whole marsh is under deep salt water when the tide comes in. They cling to the mud. It's lucky that they do. The plants make launch pads and landing pads for jumping over creeks.

There are narrow creeks that you step over like dark cracks in a pavement. The bigger ones are almost too big to leap across. Some creeks are open, with water running through them. Others are just gaps into darkness that seem to shift and open wider as you jump.

The biggest creek, the one the river makes, can only be reached by crossing the smaller ones. This creek is wider than a bus – it might be wider than two buses. Its sides go down in curves like a water slide. A smooth slope, then a level bit, then sloping down again.

An old pick-up truck is wedged in the big creek, just above the level bit.

That's where I am now. In the metal shell of what's left of the truck's cab.

The truck lies tilted, sunk so deep that if the wheels are still in place, you couldn't tell. The windows and doors are gone. The seats are half buried. There's nothing much left of them except their metal frames. The steering wheel looks almost normal. But it won't turn.

The edges of the doors are crusted with barnacles. I've seen a crab. It was greenish and small. The crab scuttled across from the door opening and disappeared into the shadows. It made me jump.

I wonder how many more crabs there are hiding, waiting for the tide.

If I look back along the creek, I can just see the flat roof of the field centre. On my left is the high bank that I scrambled down to get here. To my right is the estuary and then miles and miles of marsh. Small birds with long legs are running about like clockwork toys, searching the mud for food. The sea looks like a shred of torn silver paper out on the horizon.

I wish the sea would stay on the horizon, but it won't.

So how did I end up out here, trapped as the water starts to rise?

Chapter 2

How It Began

I didn't want to go on this school trip. I knew what it would be like.

"Come on, Jodie," said my gran. "What's the worst that could happen?"

I didn't know.

I thought the worst that could happen was coming home from school and finding the front door broken in by the police.

But it wasn't.

My brother being sent to prison wasn't.

Losing our home wasn't.

Having to move right across the country where we didn't know anybody wasn't.

So many new worst things have happened that I've given up counting them. In fact, I've given up nearly everything. I'd like to be left alone.

But Mum and Dad and Gran haven't given up. The social worker hasn't. The new school hasn't. Even my brother, Michael, who got us into this mess hasn't.

At home they prodded and prodded and prodded.

First to get me out of bed.

Then out of my room.

Next onto a bus.

After that to visit the park.

And to walk through a crowd.

To go to the shops.

Then: "School," said Mum.

This began with walking to school but not going in.

Followed by school for an afternoon. With Mum waiting in the office.

And suddenly, like falling in deep water, to school every day.

Every single day.

I didn't think I could.

"*I think you can,*" said my mum when I told her that. "Anyway, you have to."

So I did.

Mrs Nolan, my class teacher, organised this field trip. Everyone likes Mrs Nolan, even me.

Before I started at this new school, we were invited to visit for a meeting. Dad wouldn't go. He's much too shy. Gran said she was too old. But Mum isn't old or shy. She went to the meeting and she made me go too, and Mrs Nolan was there.

Mum and Mrs Nolan instantly made friends. They became a team. The get-Jodie-to-school team.

"Jodie will do well at our school," said Mrs Nolan. "I can see she's a listener."

It's clever that she noticed that, but I haven't done well. I can manage going to classes, but I can't manage anything else. I don't fit in.

And now there's this field trip.

Mrs Nolan is a Biology teacher. She told my mum she's been bringing kids to the field centre for years.

"It's free," Mrs Nolan said. "We get funding. It's part of their schoolwork. There's no barriers. I've taken students in wheelchairs. Students in care. Students speaking hardly a single word of English. There's no reason at all why Jodie shouldn't come on the trip."

"I can see there isn't," said Mum.

"It's a chance to make friends," Mrs Nolan said.

"I'll be there," Mrs Nolan promised.

But she's not.

Yesterday morning, the bus waited at school with everyone on it except Mrs Nolan.

Then a message came to Mr Morris, the other teacher who was with us. First he groaned and put his head in his hands, and then he read it aloud to the bus.

Dear Everyone,

I know that you've all been expecting me. I'm so sorry, but I won't be able to come. I've fallen off my bike and hurt my leg.
However, I absolutely trust you all to take care of each other and have a wonderful time.
I can't wait to hear about all your adventures.

With love from Mrs Nolan

Everybody began talking at once. Everyone except me. I was so stunned I was silent. What I should have done was get off that bus and run.

I wish I had, I wish I had, I wish I had. But I didn't even think of it.

So I arrived at this place on the edge of nowhere.

There was a long empty road out of a seaside town. A fast small river with a sign that said FORD NOT IN USE. An iron bridge. A single bumpy track to a car park full of noticeboards.

All the noticeboards were painted green, with black-and-white birds in the corners. Noticeboards are useful when you're on your own in a crowd, and I read every single poster. They were all warnings about tides and fires and litter.

There were no shops and no buildings except the field centre.

There was nothing but scrubby, salt-blown land and the high grassy banks that held back the sea.

Inside the field centre, it was cold. Cold from the big bare windows. Cold from the clammy floors. Cold from the wind that seems to blow all the time.

Cold from the river that loops round and out onto the marsh where it becomes this great cold creek.

The main part of the field centre is like a giant flatpack building. We were given a tour by some of the students who work there and seem to be everywhere.

The students showed us a whole block of bedrooms with lists of names on the doors. A dining room with a kitchen at one end. A big classroom they call the lab. A games room with books and a ping-pong table.

A student told us that, long ago, the field centre was just a small place where people came to see birds. It was all about birds. Visitors wrote lists of birds, and counted flocks of birds, and took blurry black-and-white photos of birds. Some of the photos are still on the walls. People even painted pictures of birds. Birds and sky and cold water. Those pictures are on the walls too.

I could see why the people who painted them didn't want to take them home.

All this happened in the old part of the field centre. The students said they took us there so that we wouldn't be tempted to go exploring on our own. No one used it any more. The rooms were damp-smelling and full of junk. One of them had a brass plate on the door. It said WARDEN. Inside, yellowing posters and notices drooped from the walls. A photo frame lay face down on a desk.

The cold was coldest there.

"All this part is haunted," said a student.

I noticed a tray of blue rat poison under a table, and I thought, *Poor ghosts*.

Chapter 3

The First Time I Heard Barking

After the rat-poison tour, a student gave us a *Meet the Team* talk in the dining room. It was to introduce us to the field-centre staff, and they also told us about the wonderful helpers, old and young, who keep this place running.

"You're sure to meet some of the helpers while you're here," the student said. "Don't forget to say hello."

Then he introduced a very scruffy person who had just rushed in. He had paint all over his jeans, his hands were black with oil, and he was wearing wellies that didn't match each other. The student said he was Martin, the boss of the field centre.

"Hi," said Martin. "Welcome, one and all. I've spent all afternoon sorting the oil-tank leak, and I've just heard there's a problem with the drains again. Please don't put wet wipes down the loos unless you are prepared to fish them out. Got to dash. Carry on."

Next came a *We Have a Few Rules for Everyone's Safety* talk.

It went on and on and on. You'd have thought we were surrounded by landmines and crocodiles instead of miles and miles of mud.

It was followed by *Hands Up for Any Questions*.

About twenty arms flew up in the air like bonfire rockets.

The student pretended not to notice the waving hands. "Before we go any further," he said, "Mrs Nolan asked me to tell you that if your name is on a list on a bedroom door, that's where you have to sleep. No swapping around. End of."

There was a lot of groaning, and all the hands fell back down again. The student ignored this too. He said that he could see we were going to be a great, super group and to give ourselves a *Wild, Wild Clap!*

So everybody did except me.

And a *Super Salty Seaside Cheer!*

Everyone did that too, while I wished I was invisible or a million miles away.

Then we were told to go and get unpacked and not to forget we were here to *Have Fun*.

But all I wanted to do was escape somewhere alone. The loudness and strangeness were more than I could bear. So I waited while everyone left, and the moment I had a chance, I sneaked outside.

I knew this broke the number-one rule they'd just told us, which was *No One Goes Anywhere on Their Own Ever.*

(But I didn't care, because what were they going to do if they caught me? Send me home?)

Once I'd escaped, I headed for a NO PUBLIC ACCESS sign that blocked a path and ducked under a stretch of red-and-white plastic tape. Then I was on a track that ran along the top of a high bank and led out towards the sea.

The bank was a sea wall that followed the line of the river. There was marshland on one side and grass and scrubby bushes on the other. It was windy, but I didn't care. I was so glad to be by myself that at first I didn't notice there was a sound somewhere ahead.

It was the sound of a little dog barking.

Oh, I like little dogs. I found one once, a curly coated puppy, trailing his lead along a path in a park. I remember how I caught him and picked him up and hugged him. I'd wanted to keep him for ever, but his owners wanted him too. They were happy I'd found him, but I was sad.

The little dog in the park had barked just like the one I heard on the sea wall that first evening.

"I'm coming," I called.

It was the first time I'd spoken since I left home that morning. My voice came out thin and was blown away on the wind.

I tried again. "I'm coming," I shouted.

Then, from behind, close behind, I heard a raspy whisper, "So am I."

I spun around.

It was an old woman. Long grey coat. Dark hat pulled down so far it shaded her eyes. Scraps of windblown, tatty hair. Worn bulgy boots creased like old bark.

I remembered the student's words in the *Meet the Team* talk and guessed this was one of the wonderful helpers he'd told us about.

Don't forget to say hello, he'd said.

"Hello," I whispered.

No reply.

The little dog was still barking. A cold fog was coming in with the tide, and birds were rising from the mudflats. All around, there were changes as the sea poured into the land.

The little dog barked again, just once, and then suddenly stopped. Like it'd been switched off.

The old woman shivered. I saw tears on her leathery cheeks.

She was looking past me, across the marsh to where the big creek was filling fast. I looked too, and I could just see the top of something: a truck roof. An empty headlight like a lost eye. A bonnet and door frame half under water.

My thoughts filled up with questions as I stared at the truck, and the old woman answered them as if I'd spoken out loud.

"Years ago, flood water swept it down and left it there."

She peered at me with her pale old eyes as if checking I understood.

So I nodded, and I waited for her to tell
me more. Who'd been in the truck? Had they
drowned? Had she heard the little dog?

But the old woman was weeping again, so I looked back towards the creek. It was almost full now and hard to see the truck any more. All at once, the wind was much colder.

When I turned again, the old woman had gone. She was far along the path.

Dark was coming and I had to go back.

Chapter 4

Listening Isn't Always Good

Just like the student told us, there were name lists on each bedroom door. The writing was Mrs Nolan's.

On the blue door I read:

Ameena and Tali
Mia
Lucy
Rachel
Jodie

I could hear them all talking as I stood outside.

First Rachel, who has a loud and bossy voice.

"They told us to bring old clothes, but all her things are new."

I knew my clothes had been noticed within seconds of me getting on the bus. My shining wellies. My perfectly puffed puffa jacket. My unfaded jeans, my matching woolly hat and gloves. Not to mention my bright new backpack, stuffed with new pyjamas, new slipper socks, new wash bag, new T-shirts, jeans and a spare hoodie. Plus a small, new, black velvet cat, just in case other people were bringing things like teddy bears.

"Black cats are lucky," my gran had said.

Not much luck so far, I thought as I listened.

"Showing off. Rich kid," said Mia, who chews her hair and chews her sleeves and always looks like she's falling to bits.

"She's not a ri …" began Rachel, and then stopped and wouldn't say any more despite being pestered.

"Your mum volunteers at the food bank, doesn't she?" Mia asked Rachel. "I saw her when we went to get stuff in the holidays. Has your mum met Jodie's family?"

"How would I know?" said Rachel.

"If Jodie goes there, it's not fair," said Mia.

"What's not fair?" demanded Lucy. I sort of don't mind Lucy. When she laughs, it sounds exactly like water running down a hole. Mrs Nolan says "Lucy, are you listening?" about twenty times a day.

"Having all new stuff and still going to the food bank," Mia explained. "It's supposed to be for people who need it. Not ones who spend all their money in Primark. She's even got new wellies. I had to bring my smelly brother's."

"Which smelly brother?" asked Rachel. "Liam or the other one? I quite like your brothers, especially the other one whose name I can never—"

"Does it matter?" shouted Mia. "We're talking about the food bank!"

We went to the food bank a lot when we first moved to this area. Before my dad got work and Mum started cleaning in the shopping centre. We haven't been for ages now. Sometimes we can even give them food. And last week my dad fished his wallet out of his jacket and said, "Jodie's going to need some kit for this school-trip thing."

I told him I didn't need anything, that they said to bring old clothes, but Dad wouldn't listen. He said, "Let's have a count-up."

Every week they put money aside for the things that matter most – train tickets (to visit Michael, my brother), rent, electric, food. In that order. Train tickets cost so much that at first the count-ups were really scary, and the food bank saved us.

But now things are better. One day when I was at school, Mum and Dad went shopping for all these new clothes. They came back so pleased with themselves there was nothing I could say.

"I don't do nightshifts at the sugarbeet factory to send my best girl off in old clothes," said my dad.

Just remembering this made me want to run home and hug him.

On the other side of the blue door the girls were still talking about food banks.

"I've never been to one," said Lucy. "Do they have a veggie option?"

"What are you on about?" asked Rachel.

"Can you choose whatever you like when you get there?" Lucy explained.

"Sort of," said Mia.

"I'd choose Black Forest gateau ice cream and fish-finger sandwiches," said Lucy.

"That's not very veggie," commented one of the twins – either Ameena or Tali. You can't tell them apart unless you have them both together, and then you can see that Tali is slightly smaller in every direction. "In fact, there are no vegetables at all."

"Cherries in the ice cream," said Lucy cheerfully. "Probably tomato sauce in the sandwich too. Do you think Jodie's lost? Had we better go and look for her?"

"She might not like it," a twin answered. "She looks angry all the time."

"She'll ask someone if she's lost," said Rachel.

"Jodie doesn't talk to anyone," said Mia.

Then all of them spoke over each other and said: "Except Mrs Nolan."

"Yes, except Mrs Nolan," agreed Lucy.

"She's Mrs Nolan's pet," said Mia.

"She's not. That's not fair to Mrs Nolan," protested Rachel.

"Well, Mrs Nolan said ..." That was one of the twins.

"It's true. Mrs Nolan did say ..." Lucy again, speaking very slowly.

What had Mrs Nolan said? What? It had all gone suddenly quiet.

"Be kind," said a twin.

I wondered if she'd said this because that's what Mrs Nolan tells us every morning: "Walk, don't run. Have an interesting day. Be kind."

"I like ..." began Lucy, after a pause, "Jodie's orange jacket."

"Tangerine," said Rachel bossily. "That's what they call that colour. Tangerine. *Had* we better go and find her?"

What if they did find me? What if they opened the door right then? *Better go in*, I thought. Get it over with, before they caught me listening.

Five, four, three, two, one, I counted down in my head and opened the door.

Then they all said, "Hi. Hello, Jodie! We were just going for supper."

And they ran.

Oh.

I didn't bother trying to unpack or anything.

After a bit, I went for supper by myself.

It was in the big room with the kitchen at one end. There were tables for six, and students from the field centre were scattered amongst the school kids. There was a student sitting with the girls from my room.

I collected my pasta and sat down at an empty table. Straight away, a student came to join me. It was the one who had given us the welcoming speech. He seemed to like giving speeches because he started another, just for me.

He began, "Hi, Jodie ..."

I froze. Why would he know my name? Who told him?

But I couldn't ask, and he carried on with his speech.

"I'm Angelo, but call me Gelo. I'm here to tell you a bit about this really special place.

It's very important for bird migration and natterjack toads, amazingly."

I decided he was weird.

"We also have a pair of short-eared owls that you might see if you're lucky. Seals too – they swim up the big creek. There's a rumour that the old warden used to talk to them. I mean, talk. Like, *talk*. And the seals understood. You can believe it if you like."

Call-me-Gelo rolled his eyes and paused for me to laugh.

"Tomorrow we have a great day planned," he went on, when he'd waited for a bit too long and I hadn't even blinked. "You'll be testing the salt levels in the freshwater lake. Then playing Botanical Bingo on the grassland. And finishing with a lugworm survey at the marsh."

Call-me-Gelo might as well have been speaking a different language.

He continued, "We may even do a colour-coded litter pick, which I promise gets quite exciting."

Call-me-Gelo had reached the end of his pasta by this time. I'd given up on mine.

"I'm going to fetch us a salad," he said. "Shall I take your plate?"

So he did, and came back with salad, chocolate milkshakes, two pink iced buns and another speech.

"There'll be a quiz tonight. You'll like that. I helped put it together, and here's a clue, I'm big time into old-school rap."

Call-me-Gelo grinned at me, living proof that death wishing doesn't work.

"The last school group brought vodka," he said. "But I think they were older than you. They struggled with the lugworms the next morning, but we did it in the end. Word of warning."

I pushed my bun towards him, and I swear he ate it whole. His jaws didn't move.

"Flapjack?" Call-me-Gelo asked next, and headed off again. So I took the chance and made a dash for the nearest door. It opened into a passage that led to the lab. There was a cupboard at one side with a PRIVATE notice on it. Inside the cupboard was a staircase. It led up to another door. There was a key hanging on a hook right beside it.

I took the key and turned the lock and opened the door. I stepped outside and found myself on the flat roof of the field centre.

I stayed there for a long time.

The wind had dropped and there were stars. I could hear no sound from below. I could have been in another world.

But far away, there was that dog again, barking, barking, barking, barking, and the air around me seemed to stir.

It was then that it came to me that I might not be alone on that roof.

I'm going, I thought. I pulled open the door, and I swear there was a movement. A turning, like a swirl of smoke or foam.

Then the noise of the other world hit me.

The corridors and bedrooms were burbling with sound. I'd missed the quiz, and they were all getting ready for bed. I found the room with the blue door and pushed it open.

"Hi," said Rachel straight away. "Tali and Ameena are sharing those bunks on the far side of the window. Me and Luce are having these ones opposite. And we've put your bag on the bed under Mia."

Oh.

"OK?" said Rachel.

I nodded and glanced at Mia, who turned her face away.

The room looked like they'd lived there for weeks. The floor was covered in stuff. I picked my way past bags and towels and hair straighteners, phone chargers and trainers and water bottles. There were a million other things, all tangled up together. Then I sat down on my bunk, way back, almost out of sight, and started listening.

Rachel was busy showing off her giant first-aid kit.

"Look," she said. "It's not just plasters and stuff like that. I've got four sizes of bandages. Slings for broken arms. Instructions for when people stop breathing, and all those packets are space blankets."

"Won't they just float away?" asked Mia.

"What?" Rachel asked.

"Space blankets in space."

"Oh, ha ha," said Rachel crossly. She got out her inhalers, her epipens and her cream for the back of her elbows. "I'm allergic to loads. Including palm oil, horses, toast but not bread, and tulips. So I have to be really careful."

"Rachel, nobody cares," said one of the twins.

The other twin said, "You can't be allergic to toast but not bread. It's not possible. If I hang my headscarf here on the door, no one's to touch it. It's new. Ameena, that means you."

"You told me twenty million times already about that scarf," said Ameena. "I wouldn't want to touch it. I hate pink."

"Cerise," said Tali.

"Pink," said Ameena. "Very, very pink. And Rachel could be allergic to toast but not bread if a chemical reaction happens in the toaster. But she can't be allergic to palm oil, because she'd be dead."

"Why would I be dead?" demanded Rachel.

"Because palm oil is everywhere," said Ameena as she accidentally fell over a rucksack. "Like the things on this floor. Ouch, ouch, ouch, ouch, OUCH! Who brought Lego?"

"Mia," said Rachel. "She's a menace. She brought a whole Lego fairy castle and a whole Lego garden."

"Why shouldn't I bring Lego?" said Mia. "If I'd left it at home, one of my sisters would've grabbed it. Anyway, I love my castle. It's my best thing."

Then she rolled off her bunk and started attaching Lego flowers onto Lego flowerbeds.

"I hate being helped," Mia said, when Tali and Ameena began attaching flowers too, but that didn't stop them.

All the time this was happening, Lucy was arranging her bed with big white pads in the bunk above Rachel.

"Luce, how many are you putting?" called Rachel.

"Three," Lucy replied.

"Three side by side or three in layers?"

"Layers."

"Will that be enough?" Rachel asked. "What if you roll about? I wish there was a way to tie you down in one place."

"That's not very kind," remarked Mia from the floor.

"I've let Luce have the top bunk, haven't I?" said Rachel. "And I know for a fact she's had two cans of Coke since she got here, so I call that very kind indeed."

"What's not kind, Mia, is you not sharing your Lego," said Tali.

"She is sharing," said Ameena.

"I am not," said Mia.

"You're all much too old for Lego anyway," said Lucy, and there was an annoyed silence. I guessed they were all holding back the words, "*You're* much too old to wet the bed!"

Instead they said, "Oh, Lucy!" and then exploded into giggles.

And private jokes and silliness.

While I listened.

Bossy Rachel. Ameena and Tali, who argue all the time. Mia with her Lego and her brother's smelly wellies. Wet-the-bed-Lucy, not embarrassed a bit – all of them part of the gang.

Friends.

That's what they were: all friends.

Only I was invisible.

"Night, Tali. Night, Rachel," said Mia.

"Night, Mia. Night, Lucy."

"Night, Ameena. Night, everyone. Oh, night, Jodie."

"Yes," they all said. "Night, Jodie. Sorry."

I never felt so lonely as in that room, that night. It was the loneliest place in the world.

I lay very quietly until they went to sleep. Then I got out of bed. There were plenty of empty bedrooms. Our school hadn't filled half of them. I thought I'd find a place for myself.

They weren't as asleep as I thought. As I closed the door, I heard Mia whisper, "Gosh, she's gone."

"Do you think she heard us talking about her earlier?" said Lucy, sounding bothered.

Yes. Of course I did.

Chapter 5

Field Day

In the morning, everything that Call-me-Gelo had said would happen came true.

We fished around in muddy reeds to fill plastic bottles with water.

Botanical Bingo turned out to be staring at circles of weedy ground and ticking off plants on our cards when we spotted things. *Dandelion*, *Daisy*, *Grass*, *Unknown*, but never the interesting things like *Orchids*, *Sea Holly* or *Wild Strawberries*.

I learned that day that lugworms look like purple hairy intestines and are very hard to love.

And also, I learned more about the history of this place.

"Why is there a car crash in the river?" asked a froggy-looking boy. He still seemed to have plenty of friends, despite his froggy-ness.

"In the *creek*," corrected Eva. She was the thin, bad-tempered student who had been landed with our group. "And it's not a car; it's a pick-up truck. There used to be a ford across the river – a shallow place where cars could cross. It's still there in fact, but people use the bridge now. The pick-up got swept away when it tried to go over the ford while the river was in flood. It was years and years ago."

"Why doesn't anyone get it out?" Froggy asked.

"They've tried, with a tractor, but it's never worked. It's much too stuck. You can't even see it sometimes. The mud banks shift and cover it right over."

"So is there an *actual* real *dead* BODY in it?" demanded Froggy. "Gross! And what a dump to be stuck in for ever."

"You might think it's a dump," Eva snapped, "but anyone who knows anything can see that it's an internationally important ecological landscape."

"Mudscape," said Froggy.

"Also," said Eva, "there are no dead bodies because the old warden driving the pick-up when it happened was rescued ALIVE."

There were groans of disappointment. Also a protest from Froggy's friend.

"The warden DIED," he said. "My dad told me before I came here. That's why everyone says this place is haunted."

"The warden died *later*," said Eva. "Ages later. Not in the pick-up truck. And anyway, I hate gossip, and I'm pretty sure it's none of your business."

Eva was skinny, but she was a fighter. She made Froggy's friend carry the lugworm buckets and shoved him on ahead. But Froggy stayed behind. Froggy had binoculars with him. He focused them on the truck and asked, "What's that in the cab?"

"You kids are sick!" Eva exclaimed. "There's nothing in the cab. Get yourself over here and carry these spades."

"It looks like a dog lead," said Froggy. "Red. One of those nylon ones, like our old dog had. I bet there was a dog in that truck and it drowned."

"Roasted lugworms have more calories than Mars bars, weight for weight," said Eva. "Much better for you too. We're going to need human lugworm tasters when we get back to the lab. Get ready for a protein snack. I'm nominating you and your friend."

"Ha ha," said Froggy. "You're joking. I bet that's not even legal."

"Ha ha," said Eva. "Of course it is. And your parents all signed permission forms about foraging before you came."

Then Eva and Froggy glared at one another, and I knew which one would win. I was right. Froggy turned away from the truck and reached out to take the lugworm spades, just as Eva had told him to do.

But Eva hadn't finished with him. "We're stopping early this afternoon," she told Froggy. "We've decided to have a talent show spectacular tonight. Everybody on stage, no excuses, anything goes, fancy dress, fire eating – if you're not too full after the lugworms. So what can *you* do? Sing?"

"Sing?" croaked Froggy.

"He can sing AND dance," said his friend, overhearing. "He can do a whole 'Circle of Life' thing from *The Lion King*. I've seen him."

"You saw me do it in Year TWO!" screeched Froggy. "I was six! I can't do it now!"

But he was too late. Already Eva was saying, "Great. That's the opening act sorted then." She wrote it down on her clipboard. "Perfect!" she told Froggy. "And what about your friend?"

"I can juggle with bananas," said Froggy's friend smugly, and then lots of other people joined in with things that they could do. All really cheerful. Having a lovely time.

I wasn't having a lovely time. I was beginning to be properly frightened. The talent show sounded brutal, and I didn't see how I could escape. I was in trouble already for swapping beds the night before.

"Can we have a chat, Jodie, please?" Call-me-Gelo and Eva had asked me after breakfast. They'd taken me aside to say, "Your school booked five rooms only, Jodie. We're going to have to ask you to move back."

I think they also had a word with the others in my room because that afternoon when we got back from the lugworms, Tali and Rachel came up to me. Smiling.

Tali said, "All of us are going to do a Fashion Parade for the talent-show spectacular tonight – that's you too, Jodie."

"Not Fashion – Fancy Dress," interrupted Rachel. "We *agreed* Fancy Dress!"

"Fashion *and* Fancy Dress," said Tali, rolling her eyes. "But Rachel's the only one doing Fancy Dress. Unless you want to as well, Jodie ..."

But I was already walking backwards so fast I hit my head against a wall. I heard Tali call, "Jodie ..." and Rachel complaining, "Now look what you've done ..." but they were too late. I'm good at vanishing, and I did.

I headed for the lab. The cupboard with the staircase. The door onto the roof.

This time I took the key with me and locked the roof door from outside.

In daylight the roof was a different place. Safe.

I only had to glance around to see that there was no one there but me.

For a long while I just sat, with my back to the locked door and my eyes screwed up against the salty wind. I thought:

I
Jodie
Alien girl
In an unfriendly world
Am safe
For a little while.

I wondered how long I had before they came and found me.

Then I wondered if there was a way off the roof. Maybe I could hang by my hands and drop. I went to look, and I saw it would be simple.

There was a wheelie-bin store built right against one side of the building below. It was solid and strong looking.

They might as well have given me a ladder.

It was the easiest thing ever to swing onto my front and drop onto the bin store. From there it took seconds to slide to the ground.

Before I knew it, I was running along the sea wall.

And once again, the barking had begun.

Oh, little dog, trapped in that truck with the rising tide.

I'm coming.

Chapter 6

Rising Tide

I turned from the field centre and ran and ran. As I did, it was as if I travelled into a picture of the past.

It was so easy to imagine the flood water at the ford. Swirling. Racing under the truck until it was lifted and swept away. Then leaving it stranded, far out on the marsh, halfway up the banks of a creek.

And soon the rising tide came. I imagined the horizon of torn silver paper moving closer. The warden pulled out just in time, before the sudden rush of salt water flooded into the cab.

And all the while, there was the frantic barking of a little trapped dog.

The silence afterwards.

I remembered the red strap of the lead that Froggy saw. It must have been fastened so tightly to the truck that years and years later it still held strong.

No wonder people said this place was haunted.

All the time I ran, the little dog barked.

Barked and barked and barked.

That old woman was on the bank too, this time ahead of me. She was shuffling along, as slowly as you walk in a dream. She knew I was there. As I overtook her, she reached out a hand.

I swerved quickly out of the way.

The old woman's voice called after me, breathless and faint. I couldn't hear the words, but I screamed back to her, "How much longer would everyone have left it, the poor little thing?

"I hate you!" I shouted as I ran. "I hate all of you! All of you! You're cruel, cruel, cruel!"

There was no one to hear. I'd left the old woman far behind. There was only me and the sea wind and the trapped little dog.

"I'm almost there," I called.

I was there.

I was far out along the sea wall. The marsh was bare, the big creek only half full of slow-moving water. The truck was high and dry.

I skidded down the bank and across the mud, with its dry grey marsh plants and pale cockle shells.

It was easy.

I jumped the little creeks, and the wider ones too until I reached the edge of the big

creek. The slope looked scary, but only for a moment. I was so nearly there that I didn't even think. I slipped and skidded down the bank and caught hold of the cab's empty door frame.

All the glass in the windows and doors was gone. The floor was deep in sea silt. The seats were just muddy shapes. But Froggy had been right. That strand of red was a dog lead. One end seemed trapped deep out of sight, but the other was fastened to a small red collar that was lying on the remains of the passenger seat. The clip that held the lead to the collar had been so long in the sea that it looked like a chunk of rusty stone.

But it looked as though I could undo the buckle of the empty collar.

For a long time, I don't know how long, the only thing that mattered to me was undoing that buckle. I had to do it, because I guessed that, once, the collar had held a frightened little dog, who had barked and barked as the tide rose around him. Who was barking still, and perhaps would always bark, unless he was set free.

It seemed that it was my task. The true reason that I'd come on this trip to a salt marsh.

"Wait," I whispered. "Wait."

There was no sound any more in the cab, except, now and then, small whimpers. I think some of them may have been me.

I broke my nails on that buckle. I skinned my fingers. I bruised them till it hurt to try again. I chewed the buckle with my teeth until I tasted blood. I prized at it with cockle shells. They broke and one of them sliced my knuckle.

But at last I felt movement. The buckle of the empty collar was beginning to give way.

Then, between one second and the next, the buckle fell apart in my hands, and the collar was open.

At that moment, there was a warmth, for the tiniest part of time. A living warmth in my hands. Then something invisible pushed into them and sprang away.

And I was quite alone in the cab, and I felt emptied out of everything. I don't know why I was crying, but I was.

A huge tiredness flooded over me. I could have fallen asleep there easily. Perhaps I did.

Then I felt a new thing. A cool wind from the sea on my face.

It woke me back into the world. Back to where I started my story.

*

The tide has turned. The river-creek is now a vast width of swirling brown water. A white swan's feather spins round and round and then begins to move upstream, towards the land.

I have to get out of this place. And I can't. I'm over my knees in silted mud. It happened while I worked on the collar. I didn't even notice.

I notice now. The mud holds me like quicksand. Like liquid concrete. I can't take the smallest step. I can't lift my feet. The bottom must have rusted out of the old pick-up truck, and I'm stuck in the creek.

The creek will fill. The marsh will flood. The small long-legged birds will take off in flocks, calling as they fly inland. The strange salt-marsh plants will be under water. My faint footprints will be washed away. The old truck will vanish.

By the time the tide is high, there will be nothing to see here but a single sheet of sky-reflecting water.

That old woman has re-appeared. She's high above, on the bank. She's clutching a bundle, hugging it close, like something found and precious.

I see the darkness of her mouth shaping words. She's speaking urgently, but not to me.

She's talking to something close, but not to me.

Then she turns to stare at me, and I catch a sound at last.

"Behind."

And I turn to look behind, and …

Oh!

A seal!

A shining seal, coming closer, closer, close enough to touch.

In all the strangeness of this day, it seems the strangest thing of all.

Faintly from the bank I hear the words, "Go quickly. Go ..."

"No, no!" I beg, but the seal turns into ripples and is gone.

And the woman is gone.

And even the swan's feather is gone.

I try to pull myself out, gripping the window frame of the wrecked truck, but something terrifying happens.

The whole thing moves.

It shifts.

In that moment, my mind goes blank with fear. If the truck rolls, I will be buried alive.

The incoming water is much colder than the water of the creek. It twirls around me in icy ribbons.

Then it's up to my waist.

Chapter 1

The Beginning and the End

My name is Jodie.

I'm on a school trip. We're at a field centre. That's a place where people study nature and geography and other outdoor things. Part of it is like a hostel and part is for science. Students from university come, and birdwatchers, as well as schools like ours. We are here for two nights. It's October, end of season, so it's cheap.

The staff said, "Anything you're unsure about, tell someone, don't keep quiet – any problems, any worries."

Some people are talkers, but I'm a listener. I never tell anyone anything.

They also said, "Nobody is to go anywhere alone."

But right from the start, I went out alone.

And now I'm trapped. I'm trapped in this haunted place.

Don't think I haven't tried screaming. Because I have.

"I'm a mummy!" says a wet face at the window.

A wave slaps hard against the cab.

"But I've unwound all my bandages."

Rachel! It's Rachel! Rachel, here!

"We'd better hurry up," she says, bossy as ever. "It's a good thing I brought my first-aid kit. It has about a million miles of bandages in it, and I think that we're going to need them all. But first I'm going to throw you Tali's headscarf ... it's a good thing it's so long. Can you catch?"

A ball of cerise pink silk comes flying in to me.

"Tie it right round you quickly," Rachel says, "and then grab this!"

She throws in a doubled length of wet bandage.

"Shove it through the scarf and knot it tight."

This is Rachel, with her inhalers, her epipens and her cream for the back of her elbows. Rachel who's allergic to palm oil, horses, toast but not bread, and tulips. It's as if she's been rescuing drowning people all her life.

"You're OK now," she tells me. "Tali and Ameena have got the other end of your bandages. Look!"

I look. Two shining figures are dressed in silver space-blanket saris and waving cheerfully back at me.

"Mia and Luce are hanging on to me, so that's fine too," Rachel says.

Lucy is hanging head-first over the edge of the creek, holding another length of bandage. It's tied to another ruined headscarf, blue this time, which is wound round Rachel.

"Hurry up, you two! My arms are breaking!" Lucy shouts. "And what if Mia lets go of my ankles?"

"I won't!" says Mia indignantly. "Rachel, do you want us to come down there too?"

"No!" yells Rachel. "Get ready to pull, all of you. Jodie, stretch out your arms. Can you reach me?"

I try, but I can't.

"Well, can you throw me the end of that red thing you're holding?"

Oh.

The dog lead. The red nylon dog lead. I'd forgotten it.

I yank it hard and nearly fall backwards as it suddenly comes loose.

"Stop mucking about!" orders Rachel. "Come on, Jodie, chuck it! This water is freezing." Then, as soon as she's got, it she shouts, "Now, everyone, pull!"

Tali and Ameena pull the bandage that's looped through the headscarf I've tied round my waist.

Rachel pulls on the dog lead.

Lucy pulls Rachel.

Mia pulls Lucy, who shrieks, "Ouch!"

And soon, in a great surging rush, I come free.

I shoot right out of the cab and into the water in a tangle of dog lead and headscarf and bandages.

A minute later and I'm in a heap on the bank with Rachel and Lucy.

Lucy wails, "Oh, Rachel, you left her wellies behind."

"Well, I'm not going back for them," says Rachel. She's pulling on the leggings that she left on the bank. Mia's yanking her sweatshirt over my head. Tali and Ameena are wrapping me in silver layers from the extra space blankets they've brought with them.

"Oh, Jodie, we searched for you everywhere!" says Lucy.

"We wanted to show you our costumes," says Tali.

"We had a space-blanket sari ready for you," Ameena tells me. "When we couldn't find you in the field centre, we went outside to look."

"We went right onto the sea wall," adds Mia.

"And we saw a seal!" says Rachel. "A real live seal, and it stared at us. And then it swam up the creek a bit and stopped and stared at us again."

"It was showing us where you were," says Mia. "Like actual magic. I always knew there was magic. But how did the seal know? Who told it?"

"What were you doing there anyway?" demands Rachel.

Before I can reply, Lucy asks, "Are we friends now, Jodie?" and then in a completely different voice she says, "I bet we've missed the talent show!"

"As long as they haven't missed us," says Rachel. She turns to look back towards the field station, and I see her hand go to her mouth, and everyone else looks too.

We are discovered, undone, tracked down. An army is racing along the track. It's led by Call-me-Gelo, but Eva isn't far behind. Then comes Martin-I'm-supposed-to-be-in-charge and a rabble of talent-show spectaculars. Last of all, there's Mr Morris.

All of them heading our way.

Chapter 8

Behind Mrs Nolan's Blue Door

Rachel doesn't stop rescuing me when the army arrives. She carries right on, starting with Call-me-Gelo. He gets to us well in the lead, shouting and waving his arms about like he's in the middle of a speech.

"Hello! Hello! Did you bring my inhaler?" Rachel demands, barging right into him. "The one I asked you to look after when we were doing that bingo stuff. Please can I borrow your hoodie? I've only got this T-shirt and I'm allergic to very cold weather. I don't know if you've noticed, but all my bandages fell off."

"What?" he shouts. "Where's Jodie? Are you all here safe? What the heck have you been playing at? Yes, take my hoodie, I suppose."

"Jodie's there, with Tali and Ameena," says Rachel, scrabbling into his hoodie and feeling in the pockets. "They've all got space-blanket saris, so they're all right. I'm a mummy. Although obviously I'm not mummified right now. Mia's a unicorn or werecat. She hasn't decided which."

"I've nearly decided werecat," Mia tells him. "I just need a face mask and a tail and a long fur coat that nobody minds me cutting up. I wondered if you would help?"

"No," says Call-me-Gelo. "No, I absolutely won't. Not a chance. Leave my pockets alone, please, Rachel, or I'm having my hoodie back!"

"We were wondering," says Tali, pushing in between him and me. "Will there be fancy-dress prizes?"

"Obviously there'll be prizes," says Ameena, also getting in Call-me-Gelo's way. "What we really want to know is, will there just be lots of smallish prizes, or will there be a great big prize for the overall winner as well?"

"This is a field centre!" complains Call-me-Gelo. "Not a flipping Amazon Prime warehouse! Have you girls lost the plot completely?"

No, they haven't. Not at all. Without Call-me-Gelo even noticing, the girls have given me the chance to get changed into more or less dryish clothes. A sweatshirt, space blankets, two pairs of socks. I pull on Rachel's woolly beanie and feel safe. I'm ready just in time to turn and smile at Eva as she arrives.

"What the flying *duck* is going *on?*" demands Eva, not smiling back. "Jodie, thank goodness! Where's the rest of your crew? And what's all this rubbish about prizes?"

"Jodie, Tali, Ameena, Rachel, Lucy, Mia, all here," says Martin-I'm-supposed-be-in-charge. He's been quietly counting heads, shooing people back along the track and gathering up dropped space blankets. "Everyone's perfectly OK. A bit wet. You'd better all have showers."

"I hate showers on a timer," says Ameena. "I wish there were bubble baths here."

"Bubble baths are very ungreen," says Tali. "There should be prizes for the shortest shower, as well as the talent show."

"There are no prizes for anything that I'm aware of," says Martin-I'm-supposed-to-be-in-charge. "Hurry up, everyone. Quick march back. Are you all right, Mr Morris?"

Mr Morris has arrived at last, puffing like a walrus. He says, "It's not good enough, people! What was the first rule you were told when you arrived here?"

"Not to go out by ourselves," says Lucy, smiling very sweetly at him. "So we didn't. What does Martin mean, there are no prizes? I thought he was supposed to be in charge."

The talk carries on as we walk back to the field centre – staff, students, a rabble of talent-show spectaculars and me.

"Gosh," says Eva as she counts us inside, "I'll be glad when you lot clear off home!"

"None of this would have happened if Mrs Nolan had been here," says Mr Morris sadly.

Which is true.

And it's also true that I escaped with no more fuss than Mr Morris saying, "Jodie, you've lost your wellies."

Which is amazing.

The talent-show spectacular goes on until nearly midnight. Everyone has prizes. They are Creme Eggs left over from Easter.

"Which Easter?" wonders Rachel in bed that night. The chocolate in nearly all of them had turned quite white. Call-me-Gelo ate Rachel's.

"Good thing he's not allergic to palm oil," says Tali.

"Don't start Rachel off," says Ameena sleepily.

"It's all right," says Rachel. "I've got my epipen. And Call-me-Gelo gave me my inhaler back too."

"Have you done your elbows?" asks Lucy.

"Yes. Have you done your—"

"It's NOT very kind to keep reminding poor Lucy that she wets the bed at night," says Mia, collecting up her Lego castle.

"I don't mind," says Lucy. "Mrs Nolan says it makes me different and interesting."

I look around the dimly lit room.

I see Tali and Ameena reach between their bunks to touch hands to say goodnight, their daily battles over. I see Rachel with her defences lined up. Inhaler, epipens, special cream, Lucy.

"We're all different and interesting," says Mia, snuggling up to her Lego castle like it's a normal thing to do.

And suddenly I know why Mrs Nolan put me in that room.

Tonight, the goodnights feel different.

"Night, Luce. Night, Meena. Night, Mia."

"Night, Rachel. Night, Tali. Night, Jodie."

"Shush," whispers Tali. "She's asleep."

Chapter 9

Morning

I wake in the grey light that comes before sunrise. Lucy is creeping about.

"Sorry," she whispers. "I just had to ... same as usual ... Oh, can I look?"

I've been clutching something tight. It's the red nylon lead with the small dog collar that I nearly drowned unfastening. My fingers have found a metal plate on it. There is writing, I am sure.

But I don't want to show it to Lucy, so I shake my head and pretend to go back to sleep until the room is quiet again.

Then I slip out of bed. I still have the roof key, and I decide I'll climb out on the roof one last time.

There's no wind thrumming through the thorny bushes. No distant bird sounds from the marsh.

No little dog barking.

And all around me, the sky is changing colour.

Blackcurrant, smoke, raspberry pink. And there's a lemonade wind beginning to blow.

I can see why Eva likes this place.

There is a name tag on the collar, and some numbers too, half lost in dirt. I am trying to make them out when Lucy appears.

"Sorry, Jodie!" she whispers. "I heard you go and I thought I'd better try to find you. In case ... I mean, after yesterday. I've been looking everywhere."

She sounds so worried I nearly hug her.

Instead, I hold out the collar.

"Oh!" she says, taking it. "It's from the washed-up pick-up, isn't it? Is that a name tag?"

I nod, and she turns it to the light and reads, "Missy".

Missy.

Missy – a little dog barking, trapped for years, every rising tide, until the buckle on her collar came loose at last. I can still feel the way she sprang from my hands – even now, under this glowing sky, in this fizzy morning breeze.

"There's a phone number too," says Lucy. "What d'you think would happen if we rang it?"

She pulls out her mobile phone and is typing in the number before I understand that she's really going to try calling it.

"Wow," says Lucy. "Listen!"

Because now there is a new sound.

Then we both run.

Down the staircase, across the lab, along to the old part of the field centre that nobody uses. Abandoned.

Abandoned, but with a landline still connected.

It rings and rings. It is still ringing when we come to the door with the old brass plate that reads WARDEN.

Then it stops.

And we stop.

Because someone inside that empty room has picked up the phone.

And I know who.

I finally understand why that old woman haunted the bank, and why she came when Missy barked. She had always come when

Missy barked, travelling back through time to the place she'd left behind.

No wonder she walked and spoke like a person trapped in a dream.

No wonder Missy leapt so swiftly into her arms.

The old woman. The old warden. The one who could speak to seals. Before she went, she waited to speak to one last seal for me.

Lucy's eyes are round with fear. She holds out her mobile to me.

I take it and breathe, "Thank you."

"Is there someone there?" whispers Lucy. "Shall I open the door? What WAS that?"

It was the sound of an old-fashioned telephone being put back on the hook.

We open the door together.

The room is just as it was before. Damp. Rat poison half eaten. Curled posters and notices drooping from the walls. Quiet telephone.

"There's no one here," says Lucy, and she's right. There is no feeling of anyone there any more.

We tiptoe around, exploring. The window looks out to the sea wall. The rat poison is cobwebbed over.

The photo on the desk is of a little white dog.

"Missy" it says underneath.

Lucy and I look at each other.

"It's all so strange," says Lucy, and I can see that she is beginning to be frightened again. "What did you hear when I gave you my mobile?

Anything? Nothing? Isn't it scary and strange? Oh, it's too scary and strange for me!"

I have to try hard to answer. It's been so long since I heard my voice out loud.

But I manage and I say, "Perhaps it's not scary and strange, Lucy. Perhaps it's just because we're interesting and different. Let's go and get the others and take them on the roof."

Which we do, and it is brilliant.

Even after Call-me-Gelo and Eva catch us there.

Afterwards, Lucy forgot that she'd asked me what I'd heard when we telephoned that number on her phone, and I never did tell her.

But I remember.

I'm good at listening.

I'd listened and what I heard was somebody far away, in a different world, listening to me.

And with them was a little dog barking.

06-06-23

Our books are tested
for children and young people by
children and young people.

Thanks to everyone who consulted on
a manuscript for their time and effort in
helping us to make our books better
for our readers.